Trouble on the Heath

Published by Accent Press Ltd – 2011

ISBN 9781907726200

The Quick Reads project in Wales is a joint venture between the Welsh Assembly Government and the Welsh Books Council. Titles are funded as part of the National Basic Skills Strategy for Wales.

Printed and bound in the UK

Cover design by www.unreal-uk.com

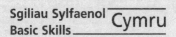

Trouble on the Heath

A comedy of Russian
gangsters, town planners
and a dog called Nigel

Terry Jones

ACCENT PRESS LTD

Chapter One

It was Nigel's favourite tree. He liked to pee on it.

Malcolm would have to wait until Nigel had finished, but he didn't mind because when you stood by this tree you got a great view of Hampstead Heath. Malcolm could imagine he was deep in the countryside, rather than in the middle of London.

There were two houses set back from the lane and, in between them, you could see one of the Highgate Ponds. Then, rising above the trees was a green hill. At the top of the hill was a circle of trees around a hump that was known locally as an old burial mound.

Malcolm knew it wasn't actually an old burial mound because he knew about burial mounds. Malcolm, you see, was Professor of History at the University of London.

But today, there was something different about Nigel's favourite tree. Malcolm frowned. There was a notice pinned to it, and notices pinned to trees are mostly bad news. They often mean that someone has lost their cat or that a loved one has died on that spot.

Malcolm peered at it more closely. It was one of those Council notices headed: "How does this affect you?" The size of the print was very small, on purpose in the hope that no one would bother to read it. Sadly for the Council, today Nigel was doing a lot of sniffing, and Malcolm had plenty of time to read it.

"Proposed demolition of two three-storey dwellings (Class C3) ..."

Malcolm looked up at the two houses. Why on earth would anyone want to knock them down? They were nice houses. OK, one of them was empty, but the other was lived in, and they were good-sized houses, too. They were probably worth a small fortune.

Still, Malcolm thought, if they were to go, there would be an even better view of Hampstead Heath from Nigel's favourite peeing tree. He – for one – would not object to that.

Malcolm couldn't tell you why he had named his dog "Nigel". But he had.

It was at that moment that Nigel vanished through the fence. This bit of road was a quiet dead-end, so it was usual for Malcolm to take Nigel off lead as soon as they got to it. It was always a relief not to have Nigel tugging at the lead, but there was always the chance that he might disappear through the fence. As he just had.

"Nigel! Nigel! Here, boy!" Malcolm called without any real hope of Nigel coming back. His lack of hope was fulfilled beyond his wildest dreams. Nigel was gone for a good twenty minutes.

After all, Nigel was chasing squirrels and such a serious task couldn't be halted simply because your master wanted it to. As any responsible Jack Russell owner knows, normal rules don't apply during a squirrel chase.

Nigel had trained Malcolm well in such matters, so Malcolm now looked around for something to do until the squirrel chase was over. He began by reading the Council Planning Notice again. Next he admired the view again. Then he started looking through the fence in the hope of seeing Nigel – the hero of the squirrel chase.

It was then that Malcolm spotted it. It was almost hidden behind a clump of weeds, down near the bottom of the fence.

It was a second, even more discreet, Council notice.

"The 'Department of Hiding Notices' probably won an award for this one," thought

Malcolm. "I wonder if they planted the weeds *after* they put up the notice?"

He moved the weeds to one side, and read: "Erection of four-storey single-family dwelling house plus two basement levels, to follow the demolition of both existing three-storey dwelling houses (Class C3)."

Malcolm took a deep breath as he took in what it said. He tried to imagine a house with four floors and a double basement standing where the two houses now stood. Cold fury welled up in Malcolm's heart. It would block the view of the pond and the Heath. He would lose his favourite view from Nigel's favourite tree!

Malcolm was trembling as he tried to find a piece of paper and a pen. Of course, that was all part of the Council's strategy. They knew that most people would not be carrying pen and paper with them when out walking their dogs. With any luck, by the time the dog walkers got home, they would have forgotten the planning application number, or even forgotten about the whole business.

And what was that at the bottom of the page in very small writing? "Comments must be received within twenty-one days of the date of this letter."

4

The date on the notice was 1st May! It was now the 18th May. That gave only three days to object.

At that moment Nigel squeezed back under the fence.

"Listen, Nigel. I want you to remember the Planning Application number: 2010/5369/CP," said Malcolm.

Malcolm was still searching through his pockets for anything that he could write on, or with. It was his habit to jot things on his shirt cuff, to the despair of his wife and the local laundry.

"Why do you do it?" his wife Angela kept saying. "You know it ruins your shirts!"

Malcolm agreed with her, but he couldn't stop himself. Especially when he needed to remember something important, like now.

However, this time his shirt was spared. His hand closed around his mobile phone. He pulled it out of his pocket and punched the planning application number into the phone's address book.

"Ha, ha! Fooled you!" he snarled at the Council with grim satisfaction.

However, Malcolm would live to regret being so resourceful, for he was about to be sucked into a web of suspense and violence that would spiral out of his control.

Chapter Two

Trevor Williams woke up in a panic.

It was a work-day, and he always woke in a panic when he had to go to work. For fifteen years he had been toiling in the Planning Department of Camden Council, and for fifteen years he had dreaded work-days.

Trevor wondered if anyone in the outside world could even guess at the horror of working in the Planning Department.

Suddenly he made his mind up. He would refuse to go in to work today. He would phone in sick. He got these migraines. Everybody knew about them. He had one today. He couldn't possibly work.

Trevor got to the bathroom and stared at his face in the bathroom mirror. He had been a young man when he'd started working in the Planning Department. Now he was old before his time. His face was lined. His eyes were dull and lifeless. Even his hair looked depressed.

He owed it to himself not to go into work today. He would go fishing instead.

Feeling much better, he shaved and made himself some breakfast: a little toast, a pot of coffee, even a boiled egg.

Then he washed up, put on his coat, grabbed his briefcase and ran for the bus. He jumped onto it just as the doors were closing, and slumped into an empty seat. He sighed a weary sigh.

More and more often he found that the only way to get himself out of bed was to pretend that he was going to phone in sick and go fishing instead.

Ah! He could feel the rod in his hand, and hear the quiet wash of the river against its banks. There was the splash now and again as fish jumped into the world above for an instant, before falling back into their watery fish-world. Just as Trevor had, for a moment, leapt from the drab world of reality into the world of his day-dreams and gone fishing.

Fish were wonderful, peaceable creatures. They minded their own business, and didn't glare at you, or write angry letters.

Fish didn't ring you up and scream abuse at you. Fish didn't threaten to take you to court or tell you that you were a Nazi working for a Nazi organisation. Nor had Trevor ever heard of fish ganging up on someone going about his normal duties, catching him outside the supermarket and pouring cold custard over his jacket. It had happened to him.

Fish didn't write angry letters about the block of flats being built outside their sitting-room window. Fish didn't accuse you of being racist because there was no letter-box outside their front door and they had to walk two hundred yards down the road to post a letter. Fish didn't harass you by ringing you every hour – on the hour – to demand to know why you hadn't replaced the trees that had been cut down by accident two years before.

And sometimes you caught fish.

That never happened with members of the public. *They* always caught *you*.

If you granted a planning application to build a really nice house with lots of rooms and a swimming pool, objectors would line up chanting in the road. They'd have their photos taken by the local newspaper, and spread rumours about the damage to the environment the house would cause. They'd claim it would upset the water table and destroy the local wild life. They'd storm the Council offices and spray green paint all over the computers. It had happened once.

On the other hand, if you refused an application to build a really nice house with lots of rooms and a swimming pool, the applicants would threaten to take you to court. They'd bring in high-powered lawyers. They would say that you weren't up to your job and that you were acting illegally. They'd phone you up and say they were going to take this matter "higher" and suggest that your job might be at risk.

There was no pleasing the General Public.

Look at that case with that supermarket a few years ago! The Council refused permission to build yet another supermarket which nobody needed. So the supermarket took the Council to court. The Council won. Then the supermarket took them to court again, and the Council won again. This went on for several years. Eventually the Council ran out of money, so they gave permission to build the supermarket.

Instead of being grateful, the supermarket then sued the Council for loss of earnings. They won, and the Council had been nearly bankrupted.

The Council, and particularly the Planning Department, just could not win.

The daily harassment, routine abuse and endless round of complaints and objections and protests would grind anybody down.

Trevor climbed the stairs to the Planning Department with a sinking heart. He opened the door and there were all the staff looking at him. Cynthia, who did the filing, was holding a cake.

"Happy Birthday, Trevor!" they all shouted.

Chapter Three

Lady Chesney was a tolerant soul. She tolerated the lowly people who jammed her sitting room at these meetings. She tolerated the off-the-peg clothes they wore. She tolerated their accents and the way they had to work for a living. She was even willing to shake hands with one or two of them, if they seemed important enough. Were any of them as grateful as they should have been? She doubted it.

That awkward young man, Malcolm Thomas, was trying to call the meeting to order. She still found it perfectly shocking that he was supposed to be a professor of something or other at the University of London. He certainly didn't look to *her* like a professor, and her opinion was worth something one would think! What was the world coming to, when a young man in a cheap suit, with a Liverpool accent, could be a professor?

Lady Chesney sighed. The country was going to the dogs. She already knew that, of course, but it was painful to see the evidence in one's own home.

Eventually the rabble became quiet, and Malcolm looked around the room.

"Ladies and Gentlemen," he said. "Fellow members of the Highgrove Park Residents' Association. Welcome to this emergency meeting to deal with the threat to demolish two houses in the ..."

"What about the Minutes?" shouted a voice from the back.

"And the Treasurer's Report?" added another.

"This is an emergency meeting," said Malcolm. "Can't we just get on with the business we've come to discuss?"

Mr Clarkson stood up. Before he'd retired, Mr Clarkson had been head manager of a mini-cab company, but he'd always fancied himself as a lawyer.

"I think they have a point. If we don't have the Minutes of the last meeting and the Treasurer's Report, this meeting could be considered in breach of the Association's rules. So, any action we decide on might be seen as invalid."

"I don't think that is the case..." began Patrick Simpson, who actually *was* a lawyer.

"I agree!" piped up Mrs Furlong. She had upset Lady Chesney by wearing a rather vulgar pair of high-heeled shoes. "I'd like to hear the Treasurer's Report."

"And the Minutes!" said somebody else.

"But the Treasurer hasn't prepared a report for this meeting," Malcolm started to explain, "because it's an emergency ..."

"Oh yes I *have*!" exclaimed the Treasurer, jumping to his feet. "I could read it out now if you like!"

"Yes! Let's have the Treasurer's Report!" said Mrs Furlong, fluttering her eyelashes at the Treasurer.

"And the Minutes!" said the same somebody else.

Malcolm sat down again with a sinking heart. He'd been chairing these meetings for the last two years and he knew what would happen next.

An hour later, they were still arguing about whether the Residents' Summer Party should be held on a Saturday or a Sunday. Finally Malcolm jumped up and waved his hands in the air.

"Please! Please!" he said. "This meeting was called to talk about the demolition of numbers

26 and 27 Highgrove Park. They want to replace them with an eyesore with fourteen bedrooms and two basements. One of these basements will contain an Olympic-sized swimming pool. Can we please just focus on that, before we run out of time?"

Lady Chesney looked at her watch and smiled. She didn't mind at all if the meeting went on longer than planned. That was because she charged the Residents' Association for the use of her room by the hour.

"I've got to go anyway," announced Major Riddington. "She Who Must Be Obeyed told me to be back by 8.00 in time for supper."

"I've just remembered we've got a dinner party!" said Paul Edgar, leaping to his feet. "My wife'll kill me!" and he dashed for the door.

Major Riddington followed him, and so did somebody else. "I only came for the Minutes," he whispered as he squeezed past Lady Chesney.

Malcolm watched them disappear, astonished. "Why do they bother to come?" he murmured.

"It's the tea and biscuits," said Barbara, the Secretary of the Residents' Association.

"But they haven't had them yet," said Malcolm.

"Then it's *not* the tea and biscuits," replied Barbara, who was always prepared to agree with anyone.

Malcolm clapped his hands for silence, as a buzz of voices had naturally followed the departure of so many members.

"The planning application in front of you explains what is proposed. The new building will be huge. Quite out of keeping with the other houses in the road ... "

Someone had raised his hand. Malcolm paused: "Yes?"

"Shouldn't we have our tea and biscuits now, before anyone else has to leave?" It was Mr Kendrick, the vet, who lived at number 25.

"Let's just talk about the threat to our environment first," pleaded Malcolm.

"But I'll have to go in fifteen minutes," said Mr Kendrick.

"But you live opposite the planned development! You're going to be the one most affected by it!" exclaimed Malcolm. "Isn't it worth a few minutes of your time to talk about it?"

"I've already written to the Council to object," replied Mr Kendrick.

"On what grounds?"

"Well … on the grounds that I don't want it."

"Is that all?" asked Malcolm.

"Well, of course. That's the only reason anyone objects," said Mr Kendrick.

"But it's not enough just to say you don't want it." Malcolm was trying to be patient.

"But I don't!" said Mr Kendrick, and there were murmurs of agreement around the room.

"None of us wants it," said Mrs Furlong.

Malcolm tried to keep calm. "We have to present the Council with a proper argument. We have to convince them that it's a bad idea to allow this development to go forward."

"I also live opposite the site. It'll spoil the view from my front room." This was Mr Kahn, who ran some sort of business from his home. No one was quite sure what his business was.

"Well, you can put that view to the Council. But I'm not sure it'll be considered grounds for an objection," said Malcolm.

"How about the 'damage to the environment'?" said Mr Kahn. "That's how I was going to put it."

"That's more like it!" said Malcolm. He turned to the rest of the room: "This is precisely why this meeting is important. We need to work out our grounds for objecting to the development. It's no good coming up with objections that the Council can ignore – because they are desperate to find ways of ignoring them."

"And there are plenty of proper grounds for objection," Malcolm went on. "The proposed development is not in keeping with the other houses in the road, which is in a Conservation Area. It is twice the size of the existing two houses put together. It will mean felling no less than forty trees and it's in a Tree Conservation Area. But there are even worse problems. Patrick, you've got some facts on the ground-water, I believe?"

Patrick Simpson, the lawyer, stood up. He was a strong supporter of the Residents' Association. "Yes, we've had a hydrological study done ..."

"A what?" put in Mr Kendrick, the vet.

"A study of the ground-water and streams in the area," said Patrick.

"Well why didn't you say?"

"I did," Patrick replied.

"I still think we should have our tea and biscuits now," Mr Kendrick said.

"I'll get Molly to put the kettle on," said Lady Chesney. She was worrying that more people might leave. She charged £1.50 for the tea and biscuits, and was counting on making enough money to buy another bottle of vodka.

"Please allow Patrick to continue!" Malcolm's voice had a whine in it now.

"Well. This second basement they're proposing ..." said Patrick.

"The one with the swimming pool?" asked Mrs Furlong.

"Exactly!"

"Will they let us use it?" asked someone.

"I don't think so," replied Malcolm.

"I wouldn't mind a swimming pool," said Mrs Furlong.

"Yes! I can't see how we can object to *that*!" said Mr Kendrick.

"Well listen!" shouted Malcolm. "Listen to what Patrick's going to tell you!"

"This second basement," continued Patrick, "will be built right across one of the underground streams in the area. The weight of the building and the way it will divert the water will flood the wild-life sanctuary on the corner. Plus we have no idea how the development might affect the ponds. It could drain them by altering the water courses and the level of the water table."

"These are strong grounds for objection to the development!" exclaimed Malcolm triumphantly.

"The Council can't ignore things like that, not in a Conservation Area," added Patrick.

"And what about the lorries?" Mr Clarkson was on his feet again.

"And the mess," said Barbara, the Secretary of the Residents' Association.

"Exactly!" said Malcolm. "With the amount of building work they are proposing, we calculate that there will be something like forty lorry movements *per day* for something like four years! The road is only three metres wide. There's just about room for a car, but a lorry will take up the entire road. There'd be nowhere for people on foot to get out of the way. So there is a serious risk of accidents."

"And where are the lorries going to turn?"

"And think about the noise!"

"And the damage to the road surface. It's a private road. We pay for its upkeep."

By the time the tea and biscuits arrived, Malcolm was quite happy with the level of outrage in the room. Lady Chesney was equally happy that she would be able to afford another bottle of vodka. The tea and biscuits triggered a buzz of conversation. Malcolm banged his teaspoon against his cup.

"OK, everybody," he said loudly. "If you've all got your teas can we carry on, please!"

"What! There's more?" asked Mr Kendrick, the vet.

"Yes, of course there's more!" Malcolm felt himself getting irritated by Mr Kendrick. There was something about the vet's moustache that annoyed him. It was so clearly based on Adolf Hitler's moustache. Had Mr Kendrick grown it on purpose as a tribute to the Great Dictator? If he hadn't, shouldn't someone have a quiet word with him?

Malcolm pulled his mind away from Mr Kendrick's moustache and forced himself to speak calmly.

"We still haven't decided what action to take," he said.

"I thought we were going to write to the Council?" said Mrs Furlong.

"Shall we each do that or will the Residents' Association write on all our behalves?" asked Lady Chesney. She did not normally join in the discussions. She felt it was beneath her dignity, but the thought of actually having to make the effort of writing a letter moved her to speak.

"Well, it would be good to do both," replied Malcolm.

"Oh!" Lady Chesney's face fell.

"But there are all sorts of other things we need to discuss, like publicity, whether we should demonstrate, who else we can get to join the protest. All that sort of thing," Malcolm looked around the faces of the members of the Residents' Association. Most of them looked dismayed.

Chapter Four

Trevor Williams sat at his desk and buried his face in his hands. It was all too much.

"They're planning yet another protest demonstration. This time it's outside numbers 26 and 27 Highgrove Park," he murmured.

"How do they have time for it?" asked Cynthia, who looked after the filing. "Don't they have jobs?"

"Not proper ones," groaned Trevor. "They're all writers and academics and bankers. I suppose they've got nothing better to do."

"It's shocking," said Cynthia. "Here we are trying to do the best for people, and all they do is moan. Moan, moan, moan."

"It's the way they hate us that gets me down," said Trevor. "It's the constant hostility, the way they look at you when they know you're from the Council. That little glint that jumps into their eyes when you say what your job is, and they reply: 'Oh! The *Planning* Department, eh?'

"What does 'eh?' mean? I'll tell you what 'eh?' means, Cynthia. 'Eh?' means: 'We're going to make your life a misery!' 'Eh?' means: 'We have complete freedom to be nasty to you.' 'Eh?' means: 'Society has given us permission to be rude to your face.' 'Eh?' means: 'Society empowers us to swear at you, to yell at you, to bad-mouth you and generally torment you and make your lives not worth living! Because _we_ pay your wages! _You_ are our servants! Our slaves! To do what we tell you!' That's what 'Eh?' means, Cynthia!"

Then Trevor Williams put his head in his hands again and started to sob. Cynthia put her arm around him and whispered something into his ear. Pretty soon, Trevor Williams put his arm around Cynthia, and pretty soon they were kissing. A little bit later they were hard at work.

It was lucky the rest of the office had all gone home.

"Happy birthday," whispered Cynthia.

Some time later, Trevor and Cynthia were sitting in a pub in Camden Town. Trevor had a pint of bitter in front of him and Cynthia a small glass of white wine.

"I often can't get out of bed in the morning," Trevor confided to Cynthia.

"That must be terrible," she replied soothingly.

"I sometimes think that God has laid his curse upon me!" Being on his third pint Trevor was in confessional mode.

"You shouldn't say such things!" exclaimed Cynthia. "Besides, you got that promotion only last week."

"Yes! 'He' really wants me to suffer! Head of Camden Planning! I ask you! The worst job in the world!"

Trevor heaved such a deep sigh it seemed to have started in his trousers. "They'll blame me for everything. They'll blame me for planning permissions granted. They'll blame me for planning permissions refused. No one ever says, 'Well granted!' or 'Well rejected!' They just complain, complain, complain!"

"But your decisions affect everybody! You save the environment! You look after conservation areas! It's important work, Trevor!" said Cynthia.

But Trevor didn't seem to have heard her. "God is punishing me for something, but I don't know for what!" He looked up at the ceiling of the pub, and cried, "What have I done wrong, God?"

As he did so, he noticed bits of chewing gum and silver paper stuck to the ceiling.

That's my life, he thought. A lot of people have worked terribly hard to produce something pointless and ugly.

"And you've got a lovely home," said Cynthia. "It's really nice."

"It's not a 'home', it's a flat," replied Trevor.

"Well, a flat can be a home, can't it?" Cynthia sounded uncertain.

"A 'home' is a house with a garden and children running around it and the smell of hot bread coming from the kitchen," said Trevor.

"Well ... you could have that if you wanted," Cynthia murmured softly. But Trevor was still staring at the ceiling.

"I wonder how they get those egg-cups made out of silver paper to stay up?" he muttered, and he didn't even notice as Cynthia reached out her hand for his.

Chapter Five

In his iron fortress, surrounded by slaves and minions, the Evil Emperor stared at the latest message from his servants in the West. There was trouble. His plans were being challenged by something called a 'Residents' Association'. What was a 'Residents' Association'? He had never heard of such a thing. He would have to look it up in the English–Russian Dictionary.

'Skulking' that was a great word! He'd found *that* in the English–Russian Dictionary. He wished he could 'skulk' more. He felt like 'skulking' now. He wanted to 'skulk' around his vast iron fortress, and see what his slaves and minions were up to, for he trusted no one.

The Evil Emperor (for that was how he liked to think of himself) lived in a world where it was unsafe to trust anybody or anything. 'Strike first!' was his motto. Strike before anyone realises you know that they're plotting against you. And one thing was always certain – people were always plotting against you.

This 'Residents' Association', for example, what could it be but a plot against him? It was clearly some sort of criminal gang devoted to taking over *his* territory. It could be that filthy creep, Ivan Morozov, his one-time partner.

Morozov was always looking for ways to do him down. He was forever scheming to take over the gambling cartels in Romania and the Ukraine.

"Pah!" The Evil Emperor spat at the imaginary Morozov. Morozov was too soft. He could never handle the rough side of the business.

Any business had its rough side, and in his particular business if that meant taking vital organs out of someone's body and replacing them with their own credit cards, so be it.

Or the rough side of business might involve kidnapping someone's mother and photographing her performing undignified acts with animals. That was just the way of the world. It was nothing to get upset about, like Morozov did. He was pathetic.

Or maybe this 'Residents' Association' was an off-shoot of the Zolkin Operation? That would be serious.

The Evil Emperor scowled. That was another great word: 'scowl'. He'd looked it up in the English–Russian Dictionary, and it fitted what he was doing now perfectly. Ah! The English language was a wonderful thing! You could always find just the right word. He only wished he could speak the language.

The Evil Emperor 'scowled' again. (You can never have too much of a good thing, he reminded himself.) If the Zolkin Operation were behind the 'Residents' Association' he would have to act swiftly. Boris Zolkin was as ruthless as he was cunning. If Boris was preparing to push his way into the UK business, then a short, sharp response was vital. It would have to convince Boris Zolkin that the Evil Emperor was even more ruthless than he was. It would have to be a deadly blow to Zolkin's ambitions in the UK. It would have to teach him never to meddle again in the Evil Emperor's affairs.

There was no question about it.

The 'Residents' Association' (whatever it was) would have to be destroyed.

Actually the Evil Emperor didn't live in 'an iron fortress'. That was just the way he liked to think of his house. It was, in fact, made of wood, and it was painted a cheerful bright blue. It had wooden pillars all around it and

29

although it was large and rambling, it was actually a very pretty house. It had been constructed in the 19th century for a wealthy landowner.

Grigori Koslov, for such was the name of the Evil Emperor, had bought it some years ago as a wreck. He had restored it with taste, and yet had managed to kit it out with all the latest stuff. It had central heating, satellite dishes, and broadband. It had a sauna, an indoor swimming pool, and a gym.

In addition the windows were fitted with bullet-proof glass and the whole building had been made fire-safe and bomb-proof. Grigori had also constructed a five-metre-high electric fence around the property. In addition three American pit bull terriers ran loose in the grounds. Grigori had researched the most dangerous breeds of dog, and discovered that the pit bull has a bite that can go through both muscle and bone. He immediately had the dogs imported from the US.

As he explained to his wife, it wasn't that he was paranoid. He just had a lot of business contacts who would like to see him impaled on an iron spike.

Chapter Six

Malcolm Thomas finished his lecture on the distribution of early Celtic fish hooks 6,000–5,000 BC. He packed his notes neatly into his bag. He nodded to the six students who had unexpectedly turned up to the lecture, and then wandered over to the porters' lodge.

His pigeon hole was surprisingly full.

The first thing he took out was a mailing from the Medieval Academy of America. He always liked getting their letters, because they had such an impressive logo. It made the study of history seem respectable again. Most people, when you told them you were a Professor of History, would look blank and say things like: "Are people still doing History?" or "I thought we already knew it all."

But you had to take the Medieval Academy of America's logo seriously. It gave the subject weight.

Then there were a dozen bills, all from the university, and addressed to "Prof. Michael Thomas, Department of History".

"You'd think they could get my name right by now," Malcolm murmured as he stuffed them into his bag.

The university had a new Managing Director, whose greatest achievement had been to change his title from 'The Principal' to 'The Managing Director'.

His second greatest achievement was to introduce a new system of accounting. Instead of the university owning the buildings, and using them for research and teaching, the new Managing Director had sold the buildings off (for a vast fortune). Lecturers and staff now had to compete on the open market to hire the lecture halls and classrooms.

Whenever a lecturer used a lecture hall, he had to pay the university out of his own salary. The lecturers' salaries were then topped-up by grants, made possible by the sale of the buildings.

The new Managing Director called the system 'Transparency in Action'. The staff called it 'Stupidity in Action'.

In addition, the new Managing Director had ordered that 'students' must now be referred to as 'clients' or 'customers'. 'Subjects' were, in future, to be referred to as 'areas of future expertise'.

Malcolm continued pulling envelopes out of his pigeon hole. There was the *History Now!* magazine. He would keep that to read over coffee. Nothing gave him more pleasure, in the whole month, than reading *History Now!* over a cup of coffee, and sneering at the articles.

But then at the bottom of the pigeon hole was an envelope that he didn't recognise. The writing was unfamiliar and it bore a Russian stamp.

Curious, he slit it open. Inside was a scrap of paper, upon which someone had written in capital letters the words: "STOP DOING WHAT YOU'RE DOING".

Malcolm thought for a while. Was the author of the note talking about teaching History? If so, Malcolm would take their advice seriously. When the new Managing Director had taken over as head of the university, he had spent a large part of his Opening Address being rude about any university teaching that did not contribute to the Gross National Product or produce some commercial break-through, like the mobile phone or soft ice-cream.

Malcolm had the distinct feeling that the teaching of Medieval History was high on the Managing Director's hit list.

If Malcolm were looking for a secure future, he should certainly stop what he was doing, but there was nothing else he wanted to do. History was his chosen subject and Medieval History, in particular, was his passion.

But he had a creepy feeling that the writer of the note was not advising him to stop teaching History.

That evening he showed the note to his wife Angela over supper.

"I received this weird note this morning," he said as he poured out two glasses of Chilean Merlot. He pushed the note across the table and watched her read it.

"One of your students perhaps?" she said, with a slight curl of the lip.

"But what are they talking about?" Malcolm took the note back, and examined it again, as he might examine a medieval manuscript. The colour of the ink, the style of the lettering, the pressure of the pen on paper, the age of the paper – all these things might give a clue as to who had written it, when they had written it, and why.

Although Malcolm was an expert in unlocking the secrets of medieval manuscripts, this scrap of paper told him nothing.

"Have you got something going with one of your students again, Malcolm?" Angela's eyes were not narrow slits at the moment, but he knew they would become narrow slits if he didn't head off this line of enquiry. He knew that once Angela's eyes became narrow slits, he would have to do a lot of soothing before they returned to their proper shape. If they remained as narrow slits for more than five minutes, his life would not be worth living for the rest of the evening.

"Of course not, my dear! You know I don't do that sort of thing!" Malcolm tried to sound as indignant as possible.

In fact Malcolm's relations with his students had always been entirely correct. But several years ago, he'd received a note in his pigeon hole which read 'I love you dearly X X X'.

Malcolm had assumed it was from Angela and had thanked her for the note at the end of the day. But Angela had not written the note. She assumed (correctly as it turned out) that it was from one of Malcolm's female students. Angela also assumed (incorrectly as it happened) that something had been 'going on' between Malcolm and the student.

In the end Malcolm had managed to persuade Angela of his innocence, but the suspicion still stayed in Angela's mind. Or perhaps it wasn't the suspicion of something that might have happened, but the fear that something might happen in the future.

"I have *always* kept my relations with the students on a professional level. You *know* that, my angel. Don't you?"

He checked Angela's eyes for any sign of narrowing, but to his relief they remained un-narrowed. He relaxed.

"Could it be the Planning Application?" she said.

Oddly, Malcolm hadn't thought about the Highgrove Park Residents' Association's latest fight, since he'd sent off their letter of objection, after the meeting at Lady Chesney's place.

"But who would have sent it?" he said, and pulled a face that meant: "Surely someone rich enough to buy both numbers 26 and 27 Highgrove Park can't also be a complete loony?"

Angela was familiar with the meaning of Malcolm's various faces, and she replied, "Just because they're rich enough to buy numbers 26 and 27 doesn't mean they're not complete loonies."

Malcolm stared at the note again, and then weighed it in his hand, as if there were some well-known connection between weight and sanity.

"And isn't the company that's bought the site Russian?" Angela added, pointing to the Russian stamps on the envelope.

"Good heavens!" exclaimed Malcolm. "But what do they mean by STOP DOING WHAT YOU'RE DOING? I'm just objecting on behalf of the Association to a planning application."

"Oh damn! There's Freddie!" muttered Angela taking a sip of the Merlot.

"I'll go," sighed Malcolm, and he got up from the table, taking his glass of wine with him, to look at their six-year-old son, who was yelling that he couldn't sleep without his submarine.

As he reached the door, Angela put her glass back on the table.

"Maybe it's one of those Russian tycoons," she said. "Maybe he's a gangster?"

Chapter Seven

Trevor Williams smelt trouble. His senses were finely tuned to trouble. In fact, if the Olympic Games held a 'Smelling Trouble over 500 metres' event, Trevor would have been a gold medallist.

It started at the back of his neck and worked its way up and over his scalp in a matter of seconds. Then it would lunge down into his tummy and produce a knot of indigestion. It would then radiate outwards towards his hands and feet, until eventually he would feel his eyes turn, as they were doing now, to the source of the 'Trouble'.

It was a mild-looking young man in a brown corduroy jacket and grey flannels. He was speaking to Cynthia, who looked after the filing.

Cynthia was following the Number One Golden Rule of the Planning Department, which was to pretend innocence. She was looking at her watch, which meant she would be telling the young man that the person he wanted to see was out of the office and wouldn't be back for some hours.

If this failed, she would move on to Rule Number Two, which would be to appeal to the visitor's sudden desire to get out of the Planning Department as soon as possible. She would do this by saying that if he left his phone number, the person he was looking for could phone him back in the comfort of his own home, when he would be sitting down with a nice glass of Chablis.

Yes! The young man was writing something down on a piece of paper that would be thrown away as soon as he left the office.

But something had gone wrong! The young man had stopped writing.

Trevor ducked down behind the filing cabinet. Damn! The young man had spotted him.

"I think your Head of Planning may have returned without you noticing," Malcolm said politely to the girl. "I'd like to speak to him at once."

Cynthia turned round to look at the Head of Planning's Office. She couldn't see Trevor.

"No, I don't think he has," she said.

"I just saw him duck behind the filing cabinet," said Malcolm pleasantly.

Malcolm actually enjoyed coming to the Planning Department. It was like reading a historical text. You had to distinguish between fact and fiction. When Julius Caesar tells us, in his *Gallic Wars*, that elks have no knees and so cannot get up if they fall over, we know it is fiction. It was exactly the same when Malcolm was told that the Head of Planning was not there, and yet he could see Trevor peering over a filing cabinet.

Trevor cursed himself. He had been meaning to get rid of the sign on the door that read 'Head of Planning'. He gave a shrug of resignation and beckoned Malcolm into his office.

"It's about this Planning Application for the demolition of numbers 26 and 27 Highgrove Park," said the young man.

"And who might you be?" asked Trevor. It was always a good idea to ask this question, since it implied that they had no business to be making the lives of honest, hard-working civil servants more difficult than they already were.

"I'm Malcolm Thomas," said Malcolm. "I'm Chairman of the Highgrove Park Residents' Association. We want to know who is lodging the Planning Application. It says on

40

the application 'Berners Ltd'. We've heard rumours that some Russian is behind it. Is that right?"

"Well, Mr Thomas." Trevor was sure of his ground here. "We know no more than you. If we receive an application from a company that's all we know too. You'd need to go to Companies House to find out who owns the company. They don't have to tell us."

"That's what I thought," said Malcolm. "It's just that one of the members of the Residents' Association has received a threatening message in the post."

Trevor gave Malcolm a sideways glance. "Really?" he said. "Are you sure it's to do with the planning application?"

"Well, not completely," said Malcolm, "but it's all we can think of. The letter had a Russian stamp, so ..."

Trevor shrugged. It was a shrug that suggested a desire to achieve great things for the public good, but a complete helplessness to do so. It was a shrug that conveyed friendly co-operation and the desire to please, but, at the same time, told of the crushing burdens of public service.

Malcolm understood all this, and turned to go. But then he stopped and asked, "By the way, what do you think of the proposed development?"

"Oh! I can't take a view. That's up to the Planning Committee," smiled Trevor, relieved at the turn the conversation was taking. He'd be rid of this person in a few minutes and then the office could get on with the real business of tea and biscuits.

"I just wondered whether you have a personal view," replied Malcolm.

"I'm not allowed to," said Trevor enthusiastically. And it was true. He had absolutely no interest in whether the proposed development was in keeping with the other houses in Highgrove Park, or whether it would ruin the ponds on the Heath, or destroy the wildlife in the area. He would never be able to afford to live in such a desirable place, so why should he care? He had to remain neutral.

Malcolm sighed. "Well, thanks for all your help," he said, and made for the door.

That was too easy, thought Trevor. I need to mix it up a bit more.

So just as Malcolm reached the door Trevor called out, "Oh, Mr Thomas! Strictly speaking I shouldn't be telling you this, but yes, I think it is a Russian company."

Malcolm nodded his thanks, and left feeling how very helpful the new Head of Planning was. He wasn't to know that Trevor Williams had a secret reason for being so helpful.

Chapter Eight

Nigel was the first there. He was closely followed by the Great Dane with only one eye called Faustus, then the Doberman called Midge. A lot of peeing went on, followed by a lot of sniffing. By the time the owners had caught up with their dogs, the dogs were busy exploring the fascinating world of bottoms. Any bottom would do, whether it was the bottom of another dog or the bottom of a hedge, fence or lamp post.

Malcolm looked at his watch. It was 10.25 a.m.

"Well, it's not quite the mass turn-out I'd hoped for," he said.

"Actually I can't stay," said Major Riddington. "I was just walking the dog. Faustus! Here boy! Can't stop. Sorry." And he continued on his way.

Malcolm turned to Midge's owner, whose name he could never remember, although he'd asked her several times. "I can't see the paper running a photo with a caption

'Angry Residents Protest' with just the two of us."

"Oh." What's Her Name? sounded crest-fallen. "Do you think anyone else will turn up?"

"I told the photographer to be here at 10.30. It's 10.26 now."

"Wait for me!" Patrick Simpson, the lawyer, came running up. "Has it all happened? Where are the others?"

"I think we are 'the others'," said Malcolm. "Not exactly a record turn-out."

"We'll just have to space ourselves out," said Patrick.

"Won't that look worse?" asked Midge's owner.

"There's the photographer!" exclaimed Malcolm. "Oh, no it isn't," he added under his breath. "It's Hitler."

"Is it really?" asked Midge's owner excitedly. She was secretly a fan of Nazi regalia.

"Mr Kendrick!" said Malcolm. "I'm glad you were able to make it. As you see we're short on numbers."

Mr Kendrick looked at them with a blank expression.

"Short on numbers for what?" he asked.

"For the mass demonstration against the development here opposite your house!" said Malcolm. He was already irritated by Mr Kendrick's presence, although he knew he shouldn't be. He had been hoping to hide Mr Kendrick behind some of the other residents. He imagined having a Hitler look-alike amongst the protesters might not win them much sympathy amongst the readers of the local paper.

"Mass demonstration?" muttered Mr Kendrick blankly.

"We voted for it at the last Residents' Association meeting," said Malcolm.

"Did we?" asked Midge's owner excitedly.

"Yes of course we did!" Malcolm could feel himself getting ruffled.

"I didn't vote for a mass demonstration," said Mr Kendrick.

"But ... but ... Anyway you're here." Malcolm was trying to control himself. "That's what matters."

"I was just going inside," said Mr Kendrick.

"But please stay!" put in Patrick Simpson. "As you can see we need everyone we can get."

"But what's in it for me?" asked Mr Kendrick.

"You live opposite the proposed

development!" exploded Malcolm. "You're the one most affected by it!"

"Look! Here's the photographer!" said Patrick.

A friendly girl in a brown bomber jacket ambled up to the group. She had a fancy SLR camera hanging from her neck.

"Hi!" she said.

"Hello, I'm Malcolm Thomas. I'm the Chairman of the Residents' Association," said Malcolm. "I'm sorry there aren't more of us."

"That's OK," replied the girl. "My name's Martha. I'm from New Zealand."

"I've got an aunt in New Zealand!" exclaimed Midge's owner. "Her name's Dancey Willis. I'm Isobel Soper."

"Isobel! Of course!" Malcolm kicked himself.

"I know Dancey Willis!" smiled Martha from New Zealand.

"You do!" cried Midge's owner. "Well isn't that a coincidence?"

"Not really. We live next door to each other. It would be difficult not to know her."

"No, I mean isn't it a coincidence that you should live next door to my aunt?"

"But we've been neighbours for years so it isn't really a ..."

"Perhaps we should get on with the photograph?" suggested Malcolm, exercising his authority as chairman.

"Are you taking a photograph?" asked Martha from New Zealand.

"Well ... er ... isn't that what you've come for?" replied Malcolm.

"Absolutely!" said Martha. "I'm going to take lots of photos. I specialise in vegetarian close-ups."

"What are they?" put in Midge's owner.

"Let's just get on with it, shall we?" suggested Malcolm.

"Is this all there are?" said another voice. It belonged to a tall man in a raincoat with greased-down hair. In fact he was the newspaper's photographer. "Not much of a protest, is it?"

"I've got to get home," said Mr Kendrick.

"Please! Please! Please stay!" cried Malcolm holding on to Mr Kendrick's sleeve. Nigel started barking at this. "Shut up! Nigel!"

"I mean, how many are there of you?"

"Five!" said Malcolm. "That's quite enough."

"Well it's not going to get on the front page," said the photographer.

"I've got things to do at home," complained Mr Kendrick.

"Please stay!" whimpered Malcolm. "Just one minute!"

"All right," said the photographer. "Try to look angry." He pulled a small Sony digital camera from his pocket.

"Is that all you're using?" said Malcolm.

"It'll do for this," said the photographer. "There! Done it!"

"We weren't posed!" exclaimed Malcolm.

"And you've got to get the site of the proposed development in the shot!" said Patrick. "It's behind you."

"Can Midge be in the shot?" asked Midge's owner.

"Yes of course! The more the merrier. Come on, Nigel!" said Malcolm.

"Wave your fists in the air!" said the photographer. "Like the girl in the bomber jacket's doing."

"What are we protesting about?" asked Martha from New Zealand.

"Got it!" said the photographer, who slipped his camera back into his pocket and wandered off.

"Don't you want our names?" Malcolm shouted after him.

That lunchtime, as Malcolm was telling the story of the disastrous protest rally and photo-shoot, the phone rang. Their six-year-old, Freddie, was the first one there. He listened and then put the phone back on the receiver.

"Who was it?" asked Angela.

"Don't know," said Freddie.

"What did they say?" asked Malcolm.

"Stop, or your kid gets it," said Freddie.

Chapter Nine

Anton Molotov hated this sort of job. For a start he wasn't very good at them. The truth is he'd always intended to be a concert pianist rather than a gangster.

Becoming a gangster had all started as a holiday job. That nice Mr Grigori Koslov had offered him three weeks' temporary work as a night-watchman. Anton Molotov had just started studying music at the St Petersburg State Conservatory.

The long vacation ran from the end of June to the beginning of September. When he found, at the end of the three weeks, that nobody said anything about leaving his holiday job, he stayed on. He was, after all, earning what seemed at the time like a fortune.

It was only in September, when he wanted to go back to the Conservatory, that he found things weren't so simple. He was told that he had to stay on as night-watchman. When he enquired why, he was told that it was because he'd seen all the stuff coming in and going out.

Now, Anton had indeed seen all the stuff going in and out of the warehouse, but he hadn't a clue what the 'stuff' was, and, being at the time more interested in music, he hadn't bothered to find out.

On 1st September he did indeed return to the Conservatory, and didn't report for night-watchman duty that night. The next day, two men came into the classroom and hauled him out, despite the protests of the teacher, and he was never allowed to go back.

"I cannot allow you, Anton Molotov, to wander around, talking to anybody you choose about what you've seen! You, who have been a witness to all our secrets!" That's what that nice Mr Grigori Koslov had said to him. Anton wanted to point out that he didn't know a thing about Grigori Koslov's secrets, but he replied, "But I want to be a concert pianist! I want to study at the Conservatory!"

"I like you, Anton Molotov," Grigori Koslov had said. "I will make sure you complete your studies."

A few nights later, when Anton was on guard in the warehouse as usual, a truck drove into the unloading bay and two men threw out a rolled-up carpet. The carpet contained none other than Vadim Volkov, who was Anton's teacher. It was he who had done all the protesting when Anton had been taken out of class.

Vadim Volkov, however, refused to speak to Anton, and sat sulking in a corner of the warehouse. Perhaps he blamed Anton for his current situation.

The next night, a lorry drove into the unloading bay. Several men in black balaclava helmets opened the back and hauled out a grand piano.

Vadim Volkov still refused to speak to Anton, but he sat at the keyboard and played for hours on end, ignoring his former pupil.

Some weeks later, when Grigori Koslov asked Anton how his studies were going, Anton explained how the teacher refused to speak to him.

The next night, Anton turned up at the warehouse to find Vadim Volkov seated, as usual, at the piano, but this time his head was missing.

From that moment Anton knew his fate was sealed. He was going to be a gangster. So he accepted his fate, because, after all, the money was pretty good. For the next few years, Anton focussed all his efforts on keeping in Grigori Koslov's good books.

And that was how Anton came to be sitting in a car in a street in north London, England, instead of on stage at the Philharmonic Hall, St Petersburg.

In his pocket was a photo of some kid and its mother. His task was to grab the kid but not the mother. That was by no means an easy job. In his experience mothers could play up pretty rough, when you tried to grab their kids. It always surprised him how violent a mother can get.

Anton remembered one bungled job, where the mother had pulled a Walther P99 semi-automatic pistol on him. He had nearly had an accident which would have meant changing his underwear, because he knew any mother who carried a Walther P99 wouldn't hesitate to fire it, if he tried to grab her kid. Still, that was back in Russia. That was the sort of thing one had come to expect these days. The fall of Communism had brought violence and organised crime, of which, of course, he realised he was part. Armed mothers were nothing new in Russia.

But this was England. People, especially mothers, didn't normally carry semi-automatic pistols around with them. This should be easy – or easier.

Anton sat for some hours, wondering what sort of supper he would get when he'd finished the job. He had just settled on going for a Tex Mex, because there weren't too many of them in Moscow, when he suddenly saw them. The mother was holding the boy's hand, as mothers do, and the boy was jumping around like he was on a pogo stick.

Anton waited until they got nearer the car. Then he calmly and deliberately stepped out of the car and walked quietly up to the woman, produced a can of Mace pepper spray from his pocket and gave her a quick squirt in the face. He then grabbed the boy's hand and whisked him into the car, while the mother fell to the floor gasping for breath.

Anton would be in South London, heading for Gatwick, by the time the mother recovered her senses.

Well, that was what was supposed to happen.

But it didn't.

Anton had parked the car slightly wide of the pavement. The result was that, when he calmly and deliberately stepped out of the car, he caught his foot on the unusually high kerb and went sprawling across the pavement right at the feet of the mother and her son.

His can of Mace flew out of his hand and went spinning across the paving stones into the gutter.

Angela let go of Freddie's hand, and knelt down to assist the man who had fallen in front of them.

"That was a heavy fall," she said to him. "Are you OK?"

"Yes! Yes!" said Anton.

"I hope you haven't twisted anything," said Angela as she helped her would-be assailant to his feet.

"He dropped this," said Freddie, and he handed over the can of Mace to his mother.

Anton made a grab for it, but was too late to stop Angela from reading the words 'Self-Defence Mace Spray'.

She looked quickly up at the man she had just helped.

Chapter Ten

"But he looked so guilty! He just grabbed the spray and drove off as fast as he could." Angela was finding it hard to persuade Malcolm that she had only narrowly escaped some sort of attack.

"But it's just a planning application, for God's sake!" said Malcolm. "Nobody's going to attack the wife of the Chairman of the Residents' Association in broad daylight."

"I don't think he was after me," replied Angela. "I think he was after Freddie. He looked at Freddie in a most odd way." Angela folded her arms.

"Freddie? No! That's too absurd!"

"But the phone call," insisted Angela. "The kid gets it!"

Malcolm frowned and fiddled with the salt cellar. "But even if the person behind the application *is* a gangster," he said, "he wouldn't warn us about what he was going to do. He'd just do it."

"When he tripped, the man swore in Russian," said Angela. She had a degree in Russian. That was how she and Malcolm had met. It was on a course in Russian that they'd both attended during one summer vacation.

Malcolm got up and walked to the window and stared out of it. It was raining, and a street light picked out the drops of rain as they burst on the pavement. He heaved a sigh.

"All right," he said at last. "I'll do a bit of research."

After all, he told himself, he was a historian. He was used to chasing up clues, checking facts, following leads, finding out why people said what they said and did what they did. There was nothing different about this. It was just happening now, instead of in the past, and it was happening to him, instead of to someone else.

He booted up his computer.

When he came down, a few hours later, he was looking very smug.

"Well?" asked Angela, although she knew she didn't need to say anything. The look on Malcolm's face meant he'd found out something. She'd seen the look before, when he'd come across some letters, written in 1399, between the Chancellor of Florence and the Archbishop of Canterbury. Or when he'd found an unknown 13th-century will or the title deeds to a house that no one had spotted before.

Malcolm sat down at the table and poured himself a glass of wine.

"Right!" he began. "The planning application is in the name of Berners Ltd. OK?"

"I'm following you so far," said Angela.

"Right!" Malcolm glanced at his notes. It was going to be a lecture. Angela also poured herself a glass of wine.

"Berners Ltd. is owned by Kostroma Investments plc. which is owned by a company called Oprosh Services which is owned by Eva Petrova Koslova. She is married to a man by the name of Grigori Koslov.

"Now, Grigori is an interesting man. In 2003 he was working for the Blackwater Company and ended up in Iraq, doing security work. In 2004 he was involved in the transfer of $1.5 billion by the Coalition Forces in Northern Iraq. The money was in $100 bills, shrink-wrapped on pallets. It filled three Black Hawk helicopters.

"The money came from the UN's Oil for Food Programme, and was entrusted to the

Americans to be spent on behalf of the Iraqi people. The courier company to which the money was handed over on the 12th April 2004 had not been properly checked out by the Coalition Forces. The money vanished. Nobody is sure just how much of it was lost, because the Coalition Forces didn't keep proper accounts! Can you believe it?

"In 2005 Grigori Koslov suddenly turns up back in Russia, a rich man. With a partner, Ivan Morozov, he sets up various gambling concerns in Romania and the Ukraine. In 2007 he is accused of trying to murder Morozov, but the police halt the prosecution for unknown reasons. In 2008 two of Koslov's men are involved in a shoot-out with two members of another company, owned by a certain Boris Zolkin, who has many police actions pending against him ..."

"In other words," Angela butted in, "Koslov is a gangster."

"In other words he is a cold-blooded, ruthless bastard!" replied Malcolm.

"I knew it!" said Angela. "That letter!"

"I don't get it," muttered Malcolm. "Why would any gangster write threatening letters? Why would he phone us to warn us that he's after Freddie? It doesn't make any sense."

Angela suddenly rose to her feet. "We've got to get out of here!"

Malcolm had the wine glass at his lips.

"Suppose they know where we live? They might do anything!"

"But it's just a planning application! It's ridiculous!" said Malcolm, and he took a gulp of wine.

Angela had grabbed a bag, and was running up the stairs. "We've got to get Freddie out of here!" She glanced over her shoulder at Malcolm. "At once!"

Some time later, they were bundling the sleepy Freddie into the back of the car. Angela suddenly grabbed Malcolm's arm so hard he dropped the car keys, and they would have fallen down the drain had Malcolm not kicked them aside as they fell.

"He's there!" whispered Angela.

"Who?" asked Malcolm picking up the car keys.

"The man who tried to kidnap Freddie ..."

"You've no proof he was trying to kidnap Freddie ..."

"But he's over there! In the black Volvo," whispered Angela.

Malcolm turned to see where she was looking. A Volvo was parked a little way up the street. Behind the wheel a dark thick-set man was pretending to read a newspaper. He looked like a gangster and not at all like a concert pianist.

"All right," murmured Malcolm. "Just act calmly and like we always go out in the middle of the night to find a hotel."

"I'm scared," whispered Angela.

"Just take it slowly."

They got into the car and as soon as Malcolm started the engine, he put his foot down on the accelerator and swung out of the parking spot, making an immediate U-turn. Luckily there was no traffic at this time of night, because he hadn't checked in his mirror. The only thing he checked was whether the man was following.

He was.

The black Volvo also swung out in a U-turn.

"I don't believe it!" muttered Malcolm. "He's chasing us! Here we are in the middle of the night being chased by a gangster, all because of a planning application!" A surge of anger gripped him. He turned and yelled over his shoulder, "Piss off!"

Freddie started crying.

"There, there!" Angela, who was also in the back of the car, put her arm around their son. "Daddy didn't mean you."

They sped down Highgate West Hill, and swung left into Swain's Lane. The black Volvo was still some way behind them. At the top of Swain's Lane, where it gets narrow, they lost sight of the Volvo because of the curve in the road. So Malcolm made a sudden right into Bisham Gardens.

"What are we doing?" whined Freddie.

"We're in the middle of an exciting car chase!" said Malcolm through his teeth. "Enjoy!"

As they sped down Bisham Gardens they saw the Volvo speed past up Swain's Lane. They'd lost him! Malcolm couldn't believe it was that simple to lose a car that was chasing you. It always seemed much harder in films.

After half an hour of zig-zagging in and out of roads he had never driven down before, Malcolm headed back to Highgate and swung along Hampstead Lane, driving round the northern edge of the Heath. As they drove past the crossroads at Whitestone Pond, they failed to notice a car parked on the other side of the pond.

The car started its engine as they continued

down into Hampstead village. It rolled forward on to the main road several hundred yards behind them. Neither Angela nor Malcolm noticed it.

"Well done!" said Angela, patting Malcolm on the shoulder.

"Was that exciting or was that exciting?" replied Malcolm.

"It was exciting!" said Freddie.

Ten minutes later they turned into the Holiday Inn at Swiss Cottage.

They checked into a family room with three beds. Freddie fell asleep immediately. Angela and Malcolm raided the mini bar, but soon followed their child's example. It had been an exciting night.

The next day, Malcolm phoned the university to say he wouldn't be coming in for the rest of the week. Then he phoned his sister, who – for some reason he never understood – lived in Leicester.

The three of them had a relaxed breakfast, and then set off, heading north.

Neither Angela nor Malcolm, nor even little Freddie, noticed the black Volvo tailing them, six cars behind, all the way up the M1.

Chapter Eleven

Grigori Koslov hadn't believed it when he first found it. It was unheard of! Why on earth would a criminal organisation post a list of all its members on its website, along with their addresses and phone numbers? Why on earth would a criminal organisation have a website in the first place?

For a split second Grigori Koslov thought that maybe he should have one too. Perhaps he also should list all his employees? Maybe it was some new government regulation?

But then he remembered who he was. He was the Evil Emperor, with a vast network of illegal businesses. He did not give a fig for the law! And anyway, the law in Russia had been a feeble, toothless pussy cat since the collapse of Communism. They couldn't force him to put up a website if he didn't want to!

But there it was. He had Googled 'Highgrove Park Residents' Association' and got their website. Unbelievable.

If it *was* an off-shoot of Boris Zolkin's organisation it must be a scam or a cover-up for some villainy.

He checked the addresses. They all seemed genuine. If he put them into Google Earth he got their exact location. He could even see the houses themselves.

But what was this?! They were all situated around the two houses he had bought! What was going on? Had Boris Zolkin positioned his henchmen to surround Grigori Koslov's property? Property which he had bought with his own hard-fought-for money?

Of course he never intended to live there, but the palace that he was going to erect in that green bit of London would act as a base for his operations in the UK. The vast mansion that he had designed himself would be a signal to Boris Zolkin and Ivan Morozov to MIND THEIR OWN BUSINESS.

It did occur to Grigori that the 'Residents' Association' might be exactly what it said it was, but such was his hatred for Zolkin and Morozov, that he simply could not believe that this wasn't their work.

In truth, Grigori had become so used to seeing the dark side of everything that he could no longer see the obvious. Suspicion and double-dealing had so deformed his mind that he had become, quite honestly, as mad as a hatter.

Only his wife, Eva, knew this, and she wasn't going to tell anyone.

Another thing Eva knew was how much their lack of a family had weighed on her husband's mind. She, herself, had no desire to have children, but Grigori had always wanted a son. That was why he had adopted that idiot Anton Molotov. Well he hadn't actually officially adopted him, but he had taken the young man under his wing some years ago, when he took him on as a night-watchman.

She could see that her husband liked the boy from the moment he first saw him. Perhaps Anton reminded Grigori of himself as a young man? They had a similar build and a similar outlook on life, except that Anton wanted to be a concert pianist back then, whereas Grigori had always wanted to be a villain. But they both wanted to reach their goals with the least possible effort.

Eva could see her husband becoming more and more fond of the young man. It was so unfair. He didn't love *her*. He never had. But she was convinced he loved Anton.

Couldn't he see that the young man was a fool? Couldn't he see that the young man was incompetent? Anyone else who worked for Grigori would have been out on their ear years ago. If they were lucky. More likely they would have quietly 'disappeared' by now.

But Grigori overlooked all Anton's defects. He forgave every bungled task. He excused the young man and encouraged him.

Slowly but surely, Grigori was turning Anton into the son he didn't have. Perhaps he didn't realise he was doing this, but Eva still felt the pangs of jealousy. She grew to hate and despise Anton in direct proportion to her husband's fondness for him.

Chapter Twelve

Malcolm normally had very little time for his sister. In fact he disliked her. He disliked her house, her hair-do and her job. She was a pattern-cutter for one of the big fashion houses in London, and in her spare time she was a dress-maker.

He disliked her general attitude. She accepted everything that happened to her with a cheerful shrug.

He disliked the way she lived. She lived amidst clutter. The real problem was that she never threw anything away. That was the thing Malcolm hated most about her. She was a hoarder.

"Glenys! Just get rid of them!" he would say as she hesitated over throwing away tins of sardines that had a sell-by date of around 1,000 years BC.

"But they may come in handy," Glenys would murmur as she loaded them back into the cupboard.

She never threw away newspapers. There

were stacks of them behind the sofa, on every seat, in the coal shed, in the pantry and (for some strange reason) even in the sink!

Glenys had been pleasantly surprised when Malcolm phoned to ask if he and his family could come and stay. She had given up expecting her brother to want to spend time with her.

"Ah, well, it's probably difficult when you've got a family," she would say to her neighbour. "I'm sure he'd come if he could."

Glenys herself had no family. She had been married for a short time, but she and her husband had not really got on together. Secretly, Malcolm was in sympathy with the husband, who also could not stand clutter.

Malcolm once told Angela: "He had wanted to throw out the newspapers, so she threw him out instead."

Glenys made a great fuss of her brother and his wife and son when they arrived. She'd baked a sponge cake, but hadn't been able to read the recipe, because she'd lost her glasses. So the sponge didn't really rise like it should have done. It was more like a large biscuit than a cake. However they ate it for tea, with the result that Glenys found her glasses. They were in the cake.

"Isn't it lucky we ate the cake?" she said. "If I'd just thrown it out I would never have found them!"

Malcolm had warned Angela not to tell Glenys why they needed to stay with her so suddenly, and since Glenys never asked, Angela had no problem staying silent. She did feel a little guilty that they might be exposing Glenys to some danger, but then she told herself that there was really no danger. They had shaken off their pursuer the previous night, and there was no way he could have traced them to this address in Leicester.

That evening Malcolm treated them all to a curry in the local Indian restaurant, rather than face Glenys's cooking again.

When they got back, they put Freddie to bed in Glenys's old work-room, and retired early.

About two o'clock in the morning they were woken by a scream.

"Freddie!" yelled Angela at the top of her voice, and leapt out of bed.

Malcolm could hardly keep up with Angela as she flew downstairs to the work-room. They flung open the door to the work-room and switched on the light.

There they stood.

Anton Molotov had one hand over Freddie's mouth and was using the other to try to restrain him.

Anton had planned to use the mace spray, but he hadn't checked it before setting off, and, when he'd pulled it out, he'd found that it was still in its plastic shrink-wrap.

Anton had cursed in Russian.

That's when Freddie had screamed. Anton had abandoned the mace canister and simply grabbed the child.

The three adults stood there frozen for a few seconds. Only Freddie kept on struggling.

Now, at this moment, something strange happened to Malcolm.

He had spent a lifetime avoiding personal danger and confrontation. He seldom got cross (except when he was reading *History Now!*). He'd always regarded himself as an easy-going sort of chap, but there was something about seeing his son struggling in the arms of a gangster, in the middle of the night, that tapped into a deep well of anger buried inside him. The anger came gushing up like an oil spill.

He flung himself at the stranger, without thinking what he was going to do. He found he had grabbed the man by his head, and his thumbs were going into his eyes. The man screamed, as he staggered back against a tall wardrobe. Freddie leapt free. The door of the wardrobe splintered, such was the violence of the attack. The wardrobe itself tottered back against the wall, upsetting the vast pile of objects that were stacked on top of it.

Amongst these objects was an old-fashioned Singer sewing machine. It dated from the 1920s, when things were still made out of first-class materials. The machine itself was made out of cast iron and it was screwed onto a heavy wooden base. It was a triumph of solid workmanship, and, when it fell, it struck Anton Molotov right on the back of his head.

In his surprise, Malcolm let go of him. Anton gave a sort of grunt and sank to his knees. But Malcolm's deep well of anger had by no means run dry, and he leapt onto the man's chest and, grabbing him round the neck, banged his head on the floor, again and again, until Angela ran forward and pulled her husband off.

They looked at the intruder.

Anton lay on the floor, not moving at all.

"Oh my God!" whispered Angela. "You've killed him!"

Malcolm was coming to his senses. The fury was spent, but he found he was trembling so much that he couldn't move.

Angela knelt over the man's body and felt him.

"He's still breathing," she said, in a tone of voice halfway between relief and regret.

"Rope!" whispered Malcolm, and he grabbed a length of cord from a pile that had fallen with all the other things that were stacked on top of the wardrobe.

In a few minutes, Anton was trussed up like a joint of meat from the butchers. He was just starting to come to.

Freddie was clinging to his father, too astonished to even cry.

At that moment Glenys appeared.

"What on earth's going on?" she asked.

Chapter Thirteen

When Grigori Koslov read the note his first reaction was cold, white fury. His second reaction was panic.

Eva watched her husband read the note with interest. She had handed it to him, having already read it herself. She smiled as she saw the waves of emotion passing through him.

She thought: I can read him like a book! No! Like a barometer!

She watched the storms of panic give way to fairer weather, as a glint of resolve entered his eyes.

The note had read: 'We have your man, Anton Molotov. We will only release him, when we hear that you have withdrawn the planning application for numbers 26 and 27 Highgrove Park.'

And there was a photo of Anton tied up and looking very unhappy.

They had Anton! Boris Zolkin had kidnapped his son! Well Anton was virtually his son, wasn't he? At that moment, it was as if a vast floodlight had suddenly been switched on. Grigori saw the world and himself clearly for the first time, and he knew, in that moment, that Anton Molotov was the only person in the whole world that he really cared about.

His wife read all this in his face, and she turned away.

If she, Eva, had been kidnapped, Grigori would have shrugged and gone on as usual. It hurt her to the quick to know that she was not as important to her husband as that … that oaf, Anton.

"Who do they think they are dealing with?" muttered Grigori. "Has Boris taken leave of his senses?"

"Perhaps it's not Boris?" said his wife.

"Of course it is! Who else would try to stop my plans?"

Eva knew there was no point in arguing. Grigori had marked his enemy. No force on earth could stop him. Only death itself.

Chapter Fourteen

Trevor Williams was heart-broken after he heard he'd won the lottery. Not even Cynthia could cheer him up.

"God has really got it in for me!" he kept saying angrily, stabbing at his lobster.

"But it's wonderful that you won!" said Cynthia, laying her hand on his arm.

"One digit! I ask you!" He glowered at Cynthia's hand. "And I'd have scooped the lot! I can't bear it!"

"But you won £20,000," said Cynthia. "That's not bad."

"One digit!" repeated Trevor. "£3 million!"

There was a silence for some moments. Then Cynthia said, "You could buy a nice car with £20,000."

"Huh!" replied Trevor. "I could buy a lot of nice cars for £3 million."

Cynthia gave up after that, and they ate their meal in a gloomy silence, punctuated by Trevor's groans and occasional murmurs of "three million" under his breath.

When he asked for the bill, the waiter returned with the manager. The two of them approached the table full of smiles. The manager bowed.

"Sir and madam, your meal this evening is on the house," he said, hardly able to contain his pleasure in giving this information.

"What?" Trevor's eyes narrowed. There was something fishy about this.

"You are our 10,000th customer, and we wish you to celebrate the fact with us! Congratulations!"

The waiter produced a bottle of champagne.

"On the house, sir and madam, of course!" said the manager, as the waiter let the cork hit the ceiling and everybody in the restaurant applauded.

As they sipped their champagne, Trevor was furious. Cynthia tried to comfort him, but it was no use. They had become the talk of the other tables.

"I hate being used for publicity like this!" he said. "I'm going to the bathroom."

As he got up he pulled his handkerchief from his pocket and blew his nose noisily. Just to show that he accepted the free meal and the champagne under protest. As he hurried off, a scrap of paper fell out of his pocket.

Cynthia picked it up. It was torn from an exercise book and it had some words written on it in capital letters. Cynthia read 'DROP THE OPPOSITION OR ELSE'.

When Trevor returned, Cynthia asked him, "Who on earth sent you this?"

The way Trevor stared at the scrap of paper and then tried to grab it out of her hand, told Cynthia all she needed to know. He hadn't received it, he had written it.

Chapter Fifteen

Glenys brought Anton his tea in bed. It had become a habit since he had become a lodger in the house.

Malcolm had argued strongly against untying his son's assailant, but both Angela and Glenys pointed out that unless Malcolm was prepared to go to the lavatory every time Anton needed to go, they would have to at least untie his hands.

But it had been Freddie who finally persuaded his father. "He's OK," said Freddie. "I like him."

Anton for his part had sworn that he would not try to escape.

"I like it here," he had explained. "I don't want to go back to my life of crime. Anyway, it was just meant to be a holiday job."

The truth is that Anton had been suffering for several years. He had been suffering from the stress of his tasks. He had been suffering from the constant fear of reprisals, and he had been suffering from knowing that he wasn't really cut out to be a villain. When he was honest with himself he had to admit he was hopeless at it.

Why couldn't Grigori Koslov see he was hopeless? Anton had seen others who had bungled a single job, and who – as a result – had ended up at the bottom of the river or fallen under an express train 'by accident'.

Why didn't that happen to *him*? Why was *he* allowed to make mistake after mistake? It wasn't fair! It put him under such strain. Was Grigori playing cat and mouse with him? Was he saving up some specially nasty end for him?

He had now been staying with Glenys for more than a month, and he hoped against hope that Grigori would forget about him.

He knew all about the demand that Malcolm had sent Grigori, because he had supplied Grigori's address. But he secretly hoped his boss would refuse to drop his planning application, so that his hosts would not have to hand him over. He wanted to go on like he was, living with Glenys and Malcolm and Angela and Freddie for the rest of his life.

He knew that was not really possible, but it was what he secretly hoped.

This morning Glenys drew the curtains for him.

"Good morning, Glenys," said Anton.

"Good morning, Anton," said Glenys. "It's another beautiful day!"

The sun streamed into the small bedroom, making the rose-covered wallpaper throw a pink glow over everything.

"I've brought you a biscuit with your tea," said Glenys.

"You're very kind," smiled Anton. "You're very kind indeed to me."

The truth was Anton had never met many people who were kind to him. His mother had been kind to him. The village butcher had been kind to him, and given him kidneys when he thought the other customers weren't looking. The village priest had been kind to him. But then Anton had realised what the village priest wanted from him in return and had run away.

That was about it, until he met Glenys.

Glenys sat at the end of Anton's bed, while he dipped his biscuit in his tea. "I thought we could motor over to Melton Mowbray and look at the pies," she said. "We could even buy one."

"A pork pie would be nice," replied Anton.

"Yes, I was thinking that too," said Glenys.

She sat there for a few moments lost in thought, and then she added, "It's funny how sometimes two people can think exactly the same thoughts at exactly the same time."

"I was just thinking that too," said Anton. "Isn't that odd?"

"Yes, it is," said Glenys.

Suddenly Angela appeared at the door of the bedroom. She was as white as the china cup Anton was drinking his tea out of.

"Where's Malcolm?" she said.

"He went for a run," said Glenys.

"Something terrible's happened!"

Chapter Sixteen

When Cynthia heard the news her heart seemed to freeze over. She had been hoping against hope that she would not have to go to the police, but now she knew she had to. She knew her duty and she refused to shirk it, even when it meant destroying her own future.

Ever since she had picked up the scrap of paper that had fallen out of Trevor's trouser pocket in the restaurant, her world had started to fall apart. Or rather the world she had hoped for had started to fall apart even before she possessed it.

She had never actually spoken to Trevor about getting married or even about how much she loved him, but every minute of every day at work had been filled by those thoughts. Every piece of filing she did was guided by whether or not she would catch a glimpse of Trevor, or whether it would involve asking Trevor a question or not.

She and Trevor had had sex, of course, but that was what you would expect in an office, wasn't it? Cynthia really didn't know, but Trevor seemed to assume that's what you did and that was good enough for her.

Somehow the sex had made it more difficult to bring up the question of how much she loved him. Nevertheless, she had seen her future as Trevor's wife and as the mother of Trevor's children. Now she was going to have to destroy that dream.

It was all the fault of those wretched Highgrove Residents. They'd started it, by objecting to some planning application. She knew how worried Trevor had been by them poking their noses into council business, and stirring up trouble. It was enough to drive anyone insane.

And that, it seemed, was what had happened to Trevor. It was the only explanation.

When she'd found the threatening note in the restaurant, she knew he had been intending to send it, but she had persuaded herself it was just a one-off. It was probably of no importance. But then she had searched the wastepaper basket after office hours, and even looked in Trevor's desk.

She had found a dozen similar notes, all threatening someone with something if they didn't stop protesting or objecting.

She felt sad that Trevor had been driven to such desperation, but she could understand how he felt. Perhaps he was just getting something off his chest. She was sure he didn't really mean any of those threats.

But now she knew he did. It was all over the newspapers and the TV.

"A wave of violence erupted last night in a quiet area of Hampstead," the newsreader had said. "During 10 minutes of mayhem, two people were killed, many wounded and one house was blown up. Police have cordoned off the area, and are appealing for witnesses to come forward."

Cynthia's heart had sunk lower with every word the newsreader spoke. How could she ignore the appeal for witnesses? She could not.

She would have to step forward and hand over all Trevor's notes. Trevor would be arrested. He would be tried and sent to prison and her future would be destroyed.

Perhaps she should ask Trevor first? Perhaps she should check if he had done all those things last night? Perhaps he hadn't? Perhaps it was just a coincidence?

But Trevor was not at work that morning. He was missing. She rang his home, but there was no answer. No one knew where he was.

If she had had any reason for excusing him, she would have held back, but she could not delude herself. She had to hand over to the police all the evidence she had.

Chapter Seventeen

"They what?" said Malcolm.

"They've blown up our house," repeated Angela.

"Our house?" said Malcolm.

"I keep telling you. Yes!"

"Who? The Council?"

"No. They don't know who. Somebody." Angela suddenly felt weary. Thank God they'd decided to stay with Glenys in Leicester. Malcolm had been talking about going back, because he was fed up with commuting from Leicester. It was an hour and a half's train ride.

"That's three hours a day!" he'd complained.

But they'd stayed on another week. Lucky them.

"Apparently a car drove down the street about 6.00 pm last night, shooting at passers-by." Angela was reading from the newspaper. "Paul Edgar was wounded in the leg. Mr Clarkson received a chest wound, and several people walking their dogs received multiple injuries. Lady Chesney was killed outright, and so was Mr Kendrick. The car drove off at high speed, and then our house exploded."

"What?! Over a planning application?!"

Malcolm sank into a chair, which had a load of dirty dishes and mugs on it. He didn't notice.

Then he muttered, "The bastards!" A blinding rage suddenly overwhelmed him.

Three days later, Malcolm found himself on a plane heading for St Petersburg.

Malcolm was not one for heroics, and normally he would have avoided any confrontation, but this was different. His wife and son were being threatened. He had to confront the man or men who were threatening them.

Nobody knew what he was up to. He didn't even know himself at first. He had cooked up an excuse about a manuscript he needed to look at in Edinburgh, and secretly booked the plane. He already had Grigori Koslov's address from Anton. All he had to do was find the man and ... and then what? Reason with him? Buy him a pair of slippers? Give him a good talking to? No.

As he sat sipping a gin and tonic, a calm came over him. He suddenly understood why he was on this plane, why he was heading for St Petersburg. He knew what his errand was.

He was going to kill Grigori Koslov.

When he first saw the house where Grigori lived, he nearly turned around and went straight back home again.

"Well, I guess I knew the guy must have enemies, but there must be some way to get in."

The house itself would have been very attractive had it not resembled a concentration camp. It was a light blue colour and built mainly from wood, with pretty pillars at the front. Around it, however, was a five-metre-high electrified fence, complete with guards who were, at that very moment, staring at him. They didn't look as if they were going to invite him in for a cup of tea.

"Think!" Malcolm told himself. "What examples from history do we have? Siege of Syracuse 214 BC? The Romans got in during some feast when the citizens were all drunk. But how will I be able to tell when Koslov is drunk? No. I know! Siege of Alexandria 1366!

Someone managed to crawl into the city through the sewage pipes, and then opened the gates at night."

But a quick tour of the drains around the house soon convinced him that that was not a practical solution. The guards were getting more and more interested in him as he circled the house. Malcolm was forced to walk away from the scene of his intended crime.

A little further down the road was a small line of shops with a run-down café. He sat himself at a table by the window, from where he could just see the main gate, if he leant forward. He ordered a black tea and sat there trying to think.

There's something obvious I'm missing, he thought. After a short while the gate opened and a car slid out and disappeared down the road.

"Maybe that's it?" he muttered. "I should let *him* come to *me*." But how could he do that? Write Koslov a letter? Say "Come and meet me or …" Or what? "Or I'll blow your house up like you did mine? Or I'll come and shoot everyone in your street?" That would hardly encourage Grigori Koslov to agree to a meeting. Even if he did meet him, he'd have tough guys hanging around, ready to pounce.

As Malcolm was thinking these things a van pulled up in front of the café, blocking his view of the gate. The side of the van bore a crude picture of a bunch of flowers and writing in Russian which read 'Courtesy Flowers, Kolpino'.

The driver came into the café and nodded at the samovar of tea. "One," he muttered.

The owner of the café poured some liquid into a cup and pushed it towards the driver along with a jug of hot water. The driver poured a tiny amount of water into the tea and leaned forward.

"I'm looking for the Koslov place," he said, as if he were proposing a drugs deal.

The proprietor of the café grunted and stuck his thumb in the direction of the blue mansion surrounded by the fence.

"Uh!" replied the driver. "Somebody's birthday," he added.

Malcolm, who had been listening to this, nearly jumped up out of his seat and ran to hug the van driver. "Of course! That's it!" he almost shouted out, but managed to restrain himself. "The Siege of Troy! The Trojan Horse!" Why hadn't he thought of it? "That's how I get in."

He put his cup down and sauntered over to the counter.

"Hi!" he said to the van driver. His Russian wasn't bad, but they would know he was foreign. "Could you give me a lift to Pushkin?"

The driver shook his head. "I only go as far as Kolpino," he said.

"That's half way," said Malcolm generously. "It'll do."

"And we're not allowed to give lifts," added the driver.

"It would save me the train fare," said Malcolm, taking out his wallet. "I'd be really grateful." He held out a few notes.

The van driver stared at them. Malcolm added a few more, and the van driver took them, paid for the tea with one of them and strode out without saying another word.

Malcolm grabbed his haversack and followed the van driver out.

"You'll have to get in the back," said the van driver. "I can't let anyone see you."

"Good idea!" said Malcolm. And he really thought it was.

As the van driver closed the doors on him, Malcolm sneezed a couple of times. The pollen count in the back of the van was so high that, if he'd been a bee, Malcolm would have thought he'd arrived in heaven. But he wasn't a bee. He suffered from chronic hayfever, and, as the van bounced over the pot-holes in the road, Malcolm started sneezing again.

Between sneezes, he felt the van stop and heard the driver explaining his mission to the guard at the main gate. Malcolm was once again overcome with sneezes, and the next thing he knew the van had stopped again, and the driver had opened the doors.

"Shh!" he hissed. "People will hear you!"

"I can't help it!" Malcolm tried to say between sneezes.

"Then you can get out here!" snapped the van driver, and he pulled Malcolm out of the back of the van. Malcolm stood there in a haze of pollen, still sneezing, as the van drove off round the corner of the house. Malcolm found he had been dropped outside a side door, out of sight of the main gate and the front door.

There was an open window beside the side door. There was also an American pit bull glaring at him from under a lean-to shed across the lawn.

Malcolm sneezed again. The pit bull hesitated for a moment, as if it didn't recognise such a command. Malcolm took his chance and ran. The pit bull ran. Curiously it didn't bark, but it ran extremely fast. However, Malcolm was at the window in half a dozen steps and, before the dog could sink its teeth into the flesh and bone of his leg, he had dived head-first through the window. He landed with a crash amongst a pile of empty jam jars.

Malcolm lay perfectly still for some minutes. The pit bull had now started barking, as it jumped up at the window, and Malcolm could hear running feet outside. It was one of the guards.

"You stupid mutt!" he heard the guard say. "You're always trying to get that pork! You can't have it!" Malcolm saw the guard's face at the window.

He lay quite still. The guard glanced in, and then slammed the window shut. "Just forget it, Fido!" he heard the guard say. "You aren't eating them joints!" Then he moved off, pulling the dog with him.

Malcolm looked around. He had, indeed, landed in some sort of pantry. There were hams and dried fish hanging from hooks. The shelves were filled with baskets of fruit ready for jam-making.

Malcolm inched himself off the empty jam jars, trying to make as little noise as possible. There was a knot hole in the pantry door, through which Malcolm peered into a large old-fashioned kitchen. There seemed to be no one around, although a large pan of fruit and sugar was bubbling on the stove. So Malcolm opened the door of the pantry and slipped quickly across the kitchen. He could feel his heart pounding, as he peered through the open kitchen door into a sort of hallway.

He could hear raised voices coming from one of the rooms. Somebody was having an argument, and suddenly the stupidity of what he was doing hit him.

A strong urge to run back to the pantry and hide seized him. What did he think he was doing? He didn't even have a plan! But running back to the pantry wouldn't solve anything.

There was what looked like a cupboard under the stairs. That would give him a few moments to think. He dashed across to it and squeezed in, closing the door quietly after him. The voices were louder and sounded angrier from here. They seemed to be coming from the room across the hall.

He tried to calm himself down. OK. Think. Think calmly.

He was in the middle of some Russian gangster's house, whom he'd vowed to kill. How? He'd strangle him with his bare hands. How do you strangle someone? Wasn't there some special trick to it? He'd never even thought about strangling anyone, apart from one or two of the historians who got their work published in *History Now!*

Calm down! Think. Maybe forget about the killing bit. Maybe he'd just come here to reason with the man, but how could you reason with someone who'd shot most of your neighbours and blown up your house, just because you'd objected to their planning application?

Then the silliness of it all hit him. The man he had to deal with was clearly insane.

"I can deal with that!" said Malcolm to himself, and suddenly he became master of the situation.

He opened the cupboard door and strode into the room where the voices were coming from.

"Good morning," Malcolm said, in Russian.

A man and a woman were standing by the window, clearly in the middle of a row. The woman was holding a bunch of flowers.

"Who is it?" she was saying, as Malcolm walked in.

"I tell you I don't know!" the man replied.

The couple turned and stared at him in surprise.

"My name is Malcolm Thomas. I am the chairman of the Highgrove Park Residents'

Association. Am I addressing Mr Grigori Koslov?" he asked in his politest Russian.

"What the fuck?!" exclaimed Grigori, in less polite Russian.

"Get lost!" snapped the woman.

"It's you?!" said the gangster.

Then something happened that Malcolm had not expected. The gangster sprang across the room and seized him by the throat.

Malcolm tumbled back onto the carpet, and the gangster was still on top of him with his fingers round his windpipe.

So that's the knack of strangling people, Malcolm found himself thinking, but Grigori was shouting at him in Russian. What was he saying?

"Where is he? You bastard! Where is he?" That's what the gangster was yelling.

"Who?" Malcolm wanted to say, but he couldn't because of the pressure on his throat.

Suddenly Malcolm found himself flailing out. He was punching Koslov in the face, and then he had his hands round his head, and his thumbs were digging into his eyes, just as he'd found himself doing with Anton.

Grigori tried to get his face away from Malcolm's fingers. Eventually he had to let go of his windpipe so that he could grab his hands to stop Malcolm poking his eyes out.

He flattened Malcolm's arms onto the floor and held them there, panting for breath.

"Who is this?" asked the woman.

"This is the bastard who's got Anton!" replied Grigori. Then he shouted at Malcolm again. "Where is he? If you've harmed one hair of his head you'll be sorry!"

"He's fine!" Malcolm could only croak his reply. His windpipe was still sore.

"I'll kill you!" screamed the gangster. "I'll kill you if you've done him any harm!"

And suddenly he was holding a gun. "I'm going to kill you anyway! But first tell me where Anton is!"

Malcolm wanted to point out the lack of logic in this demand but, in the stress of the moment, he couldn't think of the right words in Russian.

"Ahh! I'll find out anyway!" said Grigori. "Goodbye, Mr Malcolm Thomas! I'm sorry we didn't get to know each other!"

"Why?" screamed Malcolm. "Why are you doing this? All over a planning application!"

"I know you work for Zolkin!" said Grigori. "I know he is planning to muscle in on my UK operation. Well, he'll learn the hard way!" And the gangster stuck the pistol into Malcolm's mouth.

"What are you talking about?" cried Malcolm, as clearly as he could with a .44 magnum in his mouth.

"You work for Boris Zolkin! Don't deny it!"

"I've never heard of him!"

"Don't lie to me!" For a moment Grigori took the gun out of Malcolm's mouth, allowing him to say, "I represent the residents of Highgrove Park. We're simply objecting to your plans to build a monstrous house in our road and block the view of the Heath! That's all!"

Grigori stopped in his tracks. For just the slightest fraction of a second he found himself believing what this man was telling him, but it was impossible! Of course Zolkin was behind it all! Probably that creep Ivan Morozov as well! He might as well shoot the bastard at once.

He jammed the gun back into Malcolm's mouth.

When he heard the shot, the guard was drinking his thirteenth cup of tea of the day. He leapt so fast out of his seat that he spilt the drink over the table and stained his trousers.

He ran as fast as he could towards the house. The other two guards were doing the same. They all arrived in the living room at the same time.

A complete stranger was lying stretched out on the floor. His face and shoulders were a bloody mess. Sitting astride him was their boss, Grigori Koslov. His wife was standing by the open window. A curtain flapped in the breeze coming in from the garden. In the distance one of the American pit bulls was barking.

The clock on the wall ticked loudly and, it seemed, with deliberate slowness. In the centre of the dial was written "Bristol Temple Meads". Eva Petrova Koslova had bought the clock as a birthday present for her husband last year. She knew he loved anything English – even though he didn't speak the language.

At this moment, Grigori slowly toppled forward onto the stranger, who pulled himself from under him at the same time. Grigori fell with a crash onto the hard floor.

The guards turned to stare at Eva. In her hand was the gun with which she had just shot her husband's brains out. They had landed all over the stranger.

"He didn't love me!" she said. "He only loved that oaf! That idiot! Anton Molotov!"

The guards looked at each other. It had never been their policy to interfere in a domestic argument.

Chapter Eighteen

So that's really the end of the story.

Eva Petrova Koslova seemed to take a shine to Malcolm, possibly because he'd kidnapped Anton. She made him promise to keep Anton in England. That was no problem because Anton had fallen in love with Malcolm's sister, Glenys, and Glenys seemed to be happy, too. Anton and Glenys went on to have two children, one of whom became a concert pianist.

Eva was found not guilty, when the three guards swore that they had been there the whole time and that she had shot her husband in self-defence. They didn't want to lose their jobs, after all, and now Eva was in charge.

Malcolm persuaded Eva to drop the planning application and keep the two houses exactly as they were. She sold one of them to the Managing Director of Malcolm's university. In fact she liked Highgrove Park so much that she moved into the other house herself. She said she really liked the view of Hampstead Heath and the burial mound.

Trevor Williams got lucky. Before Cynthia had time to hand the threatening notes over to the police, the story of the Russian involvement in the Highgrove Park shootings was all over the newspapers and TV.

Cynthia burned all the notes and persuaded Trevor to resign from his position as Head of Camden Planning. "How can anyone be happy in a position like that?" she said to him. "It would drive anyone mad." Trevor agreed.

He also agreed to marry Cynthia, since she *had* gone to the trouble of proposing to him. And the next week he won the lottery again. Not quite the full £3 million he'd hoped for, but enough to set up a very successful business advising people on how to put in planning applications.

Angela persuaded Malcolm to resign his chairmanship of the Residents' Association, and Malcolm was more than happy to do so. He persuaded Eva to take over from him. So for the first time the Residents' Association had a chairman who knew exactly how to deal with outrageous planning applications, particularly ones put forward by Russian gangsters.

And Nigel the dog continued to pee on his favourite tree, unaware of everything.

had time to ... he heard shouts to ...
the police ... sent ... the Russian ...
... garden ... How can anyone be happy
in a position like that", she said to him. "It ...

Quick Reads

Great stories, great writers, great entertainment

Quick Reads are brilliantly written short new books by bestselling authors and celebrities. Whether you're an avid reader who wants a quick fix or haven't picked up a book since school, sit back, relax and let Quick Reads inspire you.

We would like to thank all our partners in the Quick Reads project for their help and support:

Arts Council England
The Department for Business, Innovation and Skills
NIACE
unionlearn
National Book Tokens
The Reading Agency
National Literacy Trust
Welsh Books Council
Basic Skills Cymru, Welsh Assembly Government
The Big Plus Scotland
DELNI
NALA

Quick Reads would also like to thank the Department for Business, Innovation and Skills; Arts Council England and World Book Day for their sponsorship and NIACE for their outreach work.

Quick Reads is a World Book Day initiative.
www.quickreads.org.uk   www.worldbookday.com

Other resources

Enjoy this book? Find out about all the others from
www.quickreads.org.uk

Free courses are available for anyone who wants to
develop their skills. You can attend the courses in your
local area. If you'd like to find out more, phone
0800 66 0800.

For more information on developing your basic skills in
Scotland, call The Big Plus free on 0808 100 1080 or visit
www.thebigplus.com

Join the Reading Agency's Six Book Challenge at
www.sixbookchallenge.org.uk

Publishers Barrington Stoke (www.barringtonstoke.co.uk)
and New Island (www.newisland.ie) also provide books
for new readers.

The BBC runs an adult basic skills campaign.
See www.bbc.co.uk/raw.

www.worldbookday.com

About the Author

Terry Jones was born in Colwyn Bay, north Wales, and was a student at St Edmund Hall, Oxford. He is best known for his work with the comedy group Monty Python's Flying Circus.

Terry was one of the directors of the film, *Monty Python and the Holy Grail*. He wrote, directed and starred in *The Life of Brian*, *The Meaning of Life*, *Erik the Viking* and *The Wind in the Willows*. He has also made many television programmes, including *Crusades*, *Medieval Lives*, *Barbarians* and *The Great Map Mystery*.

Terry wrote the screenplay for Jim Henson's film *Labyrinth* and is the author of many children's books. These include *Fairy Tales*, *Fantastic Stories* and *The Saga of Erik the Viking*. He also wrote the academic works *Chaucer's Knight* and *Who Murdered Chaucer? Trouble on the Heath* is his first book of fiction for adults.